How Do I Know You Love Me?

For my mummy. Thank you for showing your love every day.
And for Gabbyboodles. Thank you for our memories.
This is how you know.

- Lucy Owen

For my Mam and my Dad.
For Bibs and Bobs.
For Mamma Bear and Kel.

- Derek Bainton

First published in 2022 by Atebol Cyfyngedig, Adeiladau'r Fagwyr,
Llanfihangel Genau'r Glyn, Aberystwyth, Ceredigion SY24 5AQ
www.atebol.com

Text copyright © Lucy Owen 2022
Illustrations copyright © Derek Bainton 2022

Designed by Dylunio GraffEG

ISBN 978-1-80106-224-4

The publisher acknowledges the financial support
of the Books Council of Wales.

How Do I Know You Love Me?

Story by
Lucy Owen

atebol

Illustrated by
Derek Bainton

The bed is warm, Bear's tucked up tight.
It's time for Boodles to say goodnight.
"Love you," whispers Mummy, "I love you so."
Boodles wonders ...
"How do I know?"

"Well ...

Remember the day in the park, when we played so fast on the roundabout? I was afraid!

We climbed up the trees, wiped mud on our faces,
played hide and seek and ran silly races.

Remember the trip to the zoo? What a treat!
Gorillas and tigers we went off to meet.

But let's be quite honest,
let's be totally fair –

it was the ants and the pigeons you really loved there!

Remember the day we went down to the beach?
You chased me with seaweed, I ran out of reach.

We splashed in the rock pools
and jumped in the waves,
then bravely together
explored sandy caves.

And your birthday party on your special day,
your friends having fun, shouting hip hip hooray!

With presents wrapped up in all shapes and sizes,
cake and balloons and magician surprises.

Remember the day we did all that baking,
and the mess in the kitchen we both enjoyed making?

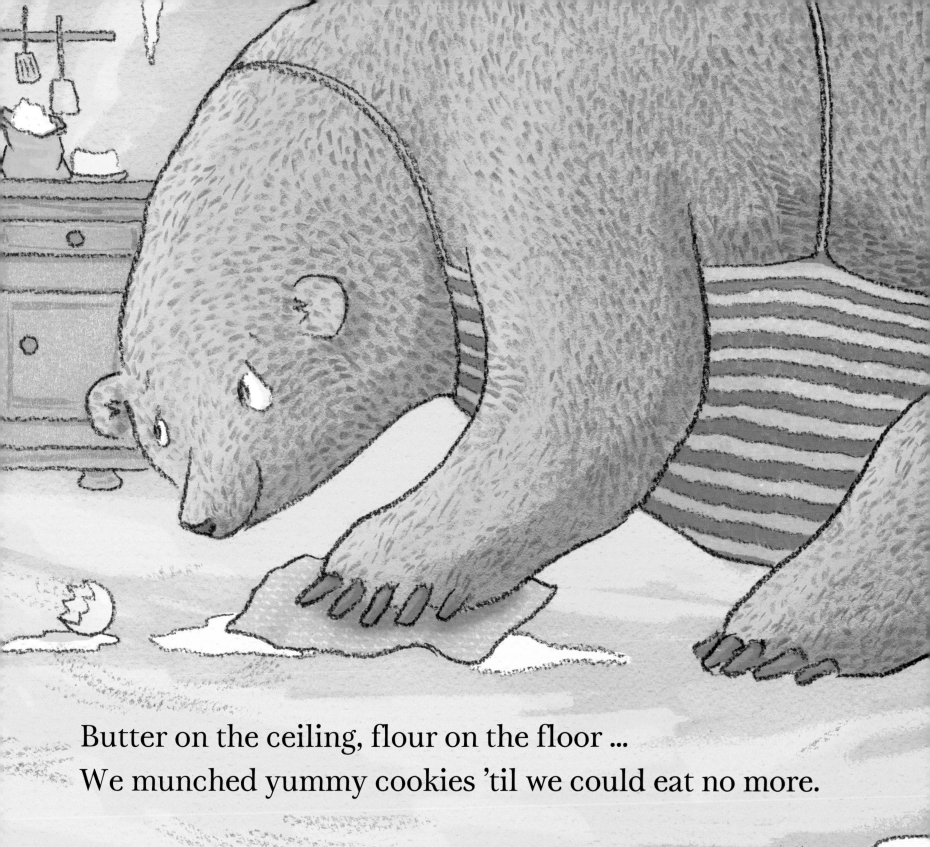

Butter on the ceiling, flour on the floor ...
We munched yummy cookies 'til we could eat no more.

And remember the night when you had a bad dream?
Monsters under the bed made you shout, squirm and scream!
Dark, ghostly shadows looked scary and creepy,

but we had a snuggle, and soon you were sleepy.

Remember the day you came home feeling sick, all covered in spots? But we knew just the trick.

Cuddles, cartoons, and Mum at your call.
We played quiet games – not so bad, after all."

The bed is warm, Bear's tucked up tight.
Happy thoughts see him through the night.
"Love you," whispers Mummy, "I love you so."
Boodles smiles ...

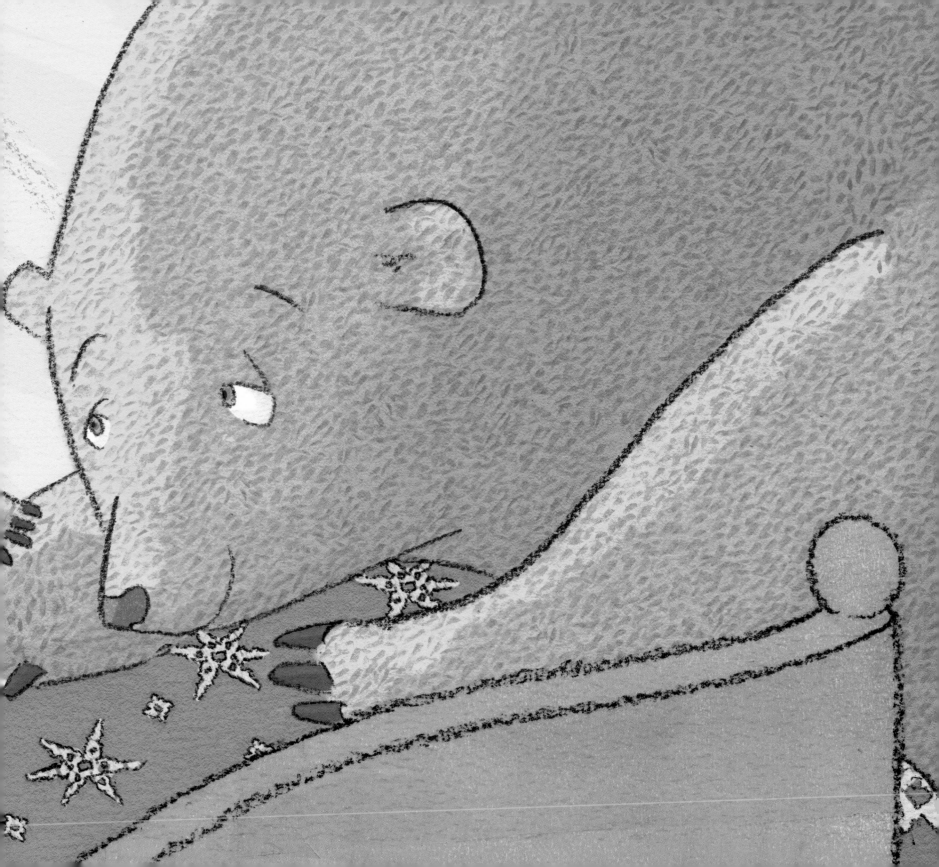

"That's how I know."